NOT *a* PLACE *to* REVISIT

STORIES

YUNYA YANG

word west press | brooklyn, ny

isbn: 978-1-7334663-7-0

published by word west in brooklyn, ny

first us edition 2023

printed in the usa

www.wordwest.co

cover & interior design: word west

Table of Contents

The Stag.. 7
A Heart That Does Not Beat............................ 17
You Will Never Need to Walk Again................... 19
The Blue...21
The Doctor Says Roots Are Growing Around Her Heart.... 31
Heritage.. 33
Perfect Vision.. 41
8. And I have never seen such savage delight since........... 49
The Warrior... 51
Rabbit.. 53
Herd.. 57

The Stag

I have been the tour guide at the Stag for almost a year. To pass the time and to have somewhere to go. Only I call it the Stag, and only in my head, though I have slipped up once or twice in conversation. I'd say, "I'll be back at the Stag by six o'clock," and Martha would frown.

I came up with the name because a stag's head hung in the living room of the house-museum. It stood out—not in the way a dead animal's head usually stands out—but in a way that it didn't fit in with the rest of the decor. The house is Victorian. The wallpaper is original, Martha told me, and so is most of the furniture. William Williams really sat in that chair, she said. She said nothing about the stag's head, though. I don't know if that's original. It looks fresh, unlike everything else that surrounds it, which smells of used towels. It's not the eyes. The eyes are false, plastic, and blind. It's the hide, sleek as if still nourished by the animal's own oil. Its mouth half-open in mid-sentence. The antlers, of course, are beautiful and menacing. It doesn't look like a severed head. It looks like a stag is passing through a wall, but time froze and it's now stuck.

The handbook Martha gave me didn't talk about the stag either, nor did it indicate William Williams to be a hunter. It talked about less important things in the house, and how Williams lived and died in it.

#

Time is slow at the Stag. Not much foot traffic at the museum, especially during winter. The townspeople have seen it already, when they were children, and this is not a place to revisit. Things rarely change here. "They are kept just as they were when Williams still lived," Martha told me.

Sometimes we get road-trippers who happen to pass through. They follow the sign on I-55, a sketch drawing of the house with "five miles to William Williams Museum, exit A-45."

A newlywed couple came to visit once. I took them around the house and told them stories, some of which I memorized from the handbook, others I made up. The guests are not supposed to walk into the rooms. All the doorways are roped off by a red velvet string. Martha wasn't there when the newlyweds came, so I unhooked the barriers and took them to every room. We tip-toed on the carpet, giggling.

"Here is where Henry proposed to Jane, Williams' only daughter," I told them when we passed the piano in the sitting room. "He died before they could get married."

The newlyweds moaned.

I'm very good at these stories. The bitter-sweet, could-have-been, wish-it-was-so ones that are prettier and more precious than happy-endings. Stories are better cut short, end before it begins, so there is no chance of spoiling.

#

I take the bus to the Stag. We only have one bus line in town, and most of the time it is empty. People drive, but I don't drive anymore. I don't really miss it. I've never understood the appeal, to grasp life in your hands like that. It's too close for comfort.

Lin Fei usually drove when we went out. I was content to be on the passenger side. "You know that's the most dangerous seat in a car," he said, "because the driver would instinctively protect himself in an accident."

"Will you protect me if there was an accident?" I asked.

"I love you," he said.

People say that so freely here. Before we moved to America, Lin Fei had never dropped that phrase so often, without care, an afterthought. He had adapted more quickly than I. Whenever he said it, I felt naked and cold.

The stag's head has no family, no one, so I offer what I can. I read the head stories from the handbook sometimes, which it enjoys. I imagine they're all old news to it, but I understand the quiet delight in distant memories. As an exchange, I've told it my past as well. It is only fair.

In that sense, we help each other.

I wish I could bring it with me everywhere I go like a friend or a car.

#

After Lin Fei died, I had no one to drive me. The Honda Civic sat in the garage for months, along with his collection of Russian dolls I'd put up on a shelf. I've sold or donated everything else he owned, but the dolls are nice. I don't take them out. I keep the smaller ones safely nestled in the bellies of the bigger ones.

I ran the car in the driveway every week to charge the battery. For twenty minutes or so, I'd read in the car as the engine breathed.

Only once I took the car out. People say that driving can be liberating, so I went for a drive. I should have done it earlier in the day when it was brighter, but I slept most hours during the day and would only wake in the afternoon when I got hungry. I went out at dusk. It was around Christmas time and the roads were empty. I drove by shining houses and saw Christmas trees through their front windows. The lights were glaring. I drove away from the neighborhood and through a forest preserve. Tall, dense spruce lined the road. It was getting darker, and I could only see as far as the headlights reached. Nothing existed until it came into view, then immediately ceased existing as it recoiled from the light. Then it was too late.

I felt the impact a couple of moments after I hit it. For a long time, I sat in the car. The engine was off and everything drowned in darkness. I didn't realize I was crying until I opened the door and the winter wind froze on my wet cheeks. My knees gave out before I could step forward. Snow was bleeding through my pants. I held onto the door handle and pulled myself up.

In front of the car was a black heap. I turned the headlights back on and saw four legs. It wasn't human. It was a deer. A dead one. Dead for a while now. Its body dried and deflated. The head was cracked open and the insides poured out like seeds from a rotten, broken watermelon.

Relief washed over me. Somebody else had killed it before me. I stepped closer to get a better look. Is this what the aftermath looked like? Instant death. With a head like that, it must have been. Was Lin Fei like a watermelon too? All popped and spilled. When the officer called about his death, he said it was quick. "No pain," he said. "If it's any consolation."

The woman didn't die. "Critically-injured" were the words. I wanted to ask how critical, but felt it wasn't my place.

She was the one driving, the officer told me. Lin Fei was on the passenger side. I almost laughed.

The car was totaled after the deer incident.

I've never driven since.

#

We had three groups in total for the whole of February. It's Friday and Martha has already left. She has to go pick up the kids because she gets them on weekends. She told me I could go home too if I want. But I don't. I don't feel strongly about staying or going. It is no difference to be here or anywhere else.

#

I sit by the window in the living room to read. I picked up reading during the time I still charged the car battery. There is no joy in it, but it offers some alternatives.

It has started snowing again. It does not fall, the snow. It runs, wanders in all directions, can't make up its mind. But eventually it lands, no matter which path it chooses.

My left arm is numb. I might have slept on it funny. Or maybe I have some sort of disease, and little by little I will lose all sensation in that arm, and beyond. Like that woman in the car. But of course I don't know what exact condition she is in, or if she has lost any feeling. I wonder if she is Chinese like us, Lin Fei and me. I wonder if she cooks.

"She drives," the stag's head says.

"Not very well," I say.

"Williams had three wives."

"How tiring that must have been."

"Not at the same time."

"Oh, I hope not."

It pauses, then says, "It's cold."

"I'll start a fire."

The fireplace in the living room still works. The stag's head is right above it and it likes to be warm.

The windows are covered by a thin layer of sweat as the fire blazes.

"It's getting dark outside," I say.

The stag's head doesn't reply. He gets in a mood sometimes, and I'll be the only one talking. But I don't mind it. I think we have some sort of understanding.

"I was in Beijing once," I say. "It was winter and snowing. Snowing so heavily. Like now, maybe even more. I had a fever and was lying on a hotel bed."

The stag's head is silent, so I go on.

"Lin Fei came to see me. He brought me some meds. I took them with hot water and was instantly cured. One moment I couldn't even lift my arm and the next I was filled with energy. We went out into the night. We walked on a cobbled, bicycle-littered hutong. There were dangling, warm street lights every hundred meters, and a smell of braised pork floating in the air. I had bad shoes on and they kept slipping, so Lin Fei half-carried me on his arm. I put my hand in his coat pocket and felt the bumpy little cotton balls inside."

"It snows in Beijing?"

"Yes. It was the first time I've seen snow. I'm not from there, you see."

"You're not from here, either."

"No."

"You move."

"Yes, well. I don't, not really."

"Where were you going?"

"A house. Somebody's house. A set of stone lions guarded the red doors. Lin Fei knocked and we were let in. There were tables and chairs set up in a small, square yard. A fire going in a brazier. We sat down. Our host served us the most delicious food. Fish head, duck blood soup, and venison stew." I glance at the stag's head. "Sorry."

"I remember when I was in love," it says.

The fire is dying down.

"I should go," I say. "Or I'll miss the last bus."

#

The snow is knee-high and still coming. The bus is late. I hop from foot to foot for another twenty minutes and still no sign of the bus.

Static buzzes from the rusty speaker hanging on a pole:

"…vehicle collision on the bus route. The bus is canceled. We apologize for the inconvenience caused…Dear passengers, there is a vehicle collision…"

I can't tell where the road starts and where the sidewalk ends. Snow settles on everything. I wait for the canceled bus for another ten minutes. It's not as cold anymore now. My face is heating up. My toes are warm in my boots, the wet socks have dried, though of course, they couldn't have. Snow shines everywhere and it is bright, almost blinding, under the sunny street light.

I've decided to go back to the Stag. I can stay the night there and leave in the morning.

I go into the house from the front door. This is the first time I've used it. Martha is very particular about only using the side door. "So as not to disturb the house," she said.

But houses are better disturbed. A house that's not disturbed is a dead one, which I guess the Stag is, but even so.

I open the double doors and step in. I've never noticed the small chandelier on the ceiling of the vestibule before. It's copper-red, with rubies dangling on its arms.

"You're back," the stag's head's voice travels from the living room.

"Yes. The bus is canceled. I'm staying the night." I sit on the bench to take off my boots. Williams must have done the same thing, every night when he came home, sitting on this exact bench to take off his shoes as one of the three wives beckoned him in. A fire would blaze somewhere and it'd be warm in the house. Dinner would be set in the dining room, silverware laid on each side of the stacked plates. A smell of something delightful brewing on the stove.

"I'm home," he'd say.

"He rarely came home," the stag's head says. "He had business elsewhere."

"What about the food?" I ask. "It will get cold."

"His wives cried a great deal."

"I must not cry."

But tears are slinking down my cheeks as I restart the fire, the smoke stinging my eyes.

The stag's head seems to melt.

"Is it too warm for you?" I ask.

"It's never warm enough."

I touch its fur. A terrible and wonderful heat is spilling from it, and as I stroke it, it starts to tremble.

I must do something. I must make it feel the warmth.

I grab the iron poker, the burning handle sears my skin, and a pleasant pain blooms in my palms. I swing it up and hammer hard on the wall above the fireplace. It cracks, the wall. I keep going. Each time I strike something thaws within me, and a feverish tide is raging, rolling, rising in my chest. The stag's body drives through the crumbling bricks, its muscles flexing and freeing from the feeble barrier that used to bind it. Inch by inch, it emerges from the yielding wall, hooves digging into the fire, neck stretching long, a roar releasing from the pit of its throat. It is charging forward, forward, forward towards me, and together we enter the home of eternal summers.

A Heart That Does Not Beat

The old woman walks on the beach barefoot. It is winter and deserted. She stays close to the water, so when the tide rolls in, it touches her skin. Years ago, she scattered her husband's ashes in the sea. Not in this sea, but all seas are connected. She is on land, however, which is unfortunate.

#

Chang'e flew to the moon after she became immortal. She wanted to live but didn't know the consequences of living. She has a palace on the moon. It is vast and cold. She has a rabbit. It is also immortal and its heart does not beat. She plants a sweet olive tree.

#

When the old woman was a young girl, she lived on a different land, where sweet olive trees bloomed. Her husband used to bring the flowers home and arrange them in a chipped vase on the kitchen table. She no longer remembers their fragrance, but if she smells them again, she is sure she would recognize it.

#

Chang'e wishes there was a bridge between the moon and the earth. She wishes for a fantastic collision between time and distance. Her sweet olive tree grows. It is unattended, yet it survives.

You Will Never Need to Walk Again

With a strip of long, cream-colored cloth, her feet are wrapped, toes crushed, joints snapped. Tighter and narrower, the bind gains with each passing day, her pain boils and burns. At night, she lies unsleeping, unseeing, biting down at the crook of her thumb and pressing her purple feet against the soothing, chilling wall. Poets sing the beauty of small feet, curved as the crescent moon, delicate like a golden lotus floating on a pond. How lovely she walks in those pointed, embroidered little shoes! She imagines that Cinderella bound her own feet, bamboo chips to sculpt the shape, porcelain shards to cut the bone, peony powder to cover the sweet, rotten smell, the betraying blood seeping from her wounds. As she descends the grand stairs, her body sways with each step like the sickly branches of a willow tree, and with each step the pain streaks through her, before she crumbles on the palm of a prince.

The Blue

Lanlan is ten and enlightened. Brimming with knowledge. No longer lost. It is a terrible thing.

Lanlan and her father and Kitty Cassidy are staying in a blue house for the summer. The house is on an island seven miles east of the coast facing the Atlantic, which is a little less blue than the house. She sleeps in the attic. She picked the room because she could hear the weather vane turning through the slanted ceiling.

"You have such fascinating perspectives, Lanlan, sweetheart," Kitty says.

Lanlan forgives her for saying such things. Kitty is not enlightened. She lives down below, her feet firmly on the ground. She ends her sentences with periods, even when it is a question. Lanlan resents that sense of security, but her father loves it. Her mother once told her a story about a crow filling up a bottle with pebbles in order to drink the water from it. We all want to be filled by small stones. There is water in all of us, and we all want to reach it.

Kitty is kind to Lanlan. She is not her mother

and therefore does not read her fables or fairy tales, but she holds her hand when they take their evening walks. Kitty's hands are always warm and lathered by a lavender-scented hand cream. They are improbably smooth. If Lanlan had put her lips on Kitty's palm, she would not feel the lines of her skin. When Lanlan was small, she used to bring a thin, pink towel to bed every night, rub her lips on its rough edges, feel their pulsing caress.

She can be Kitty's friend, but she cannot kiss her palm.

#

Kitty has gotten Lanlan's father into scuba-diving. She loves the water. She was born in a coastal town where mothers gave birth in bathtubs and kids knew how to swim since infancy. She tells Lanlan that she once swam next to a shark whose bloodshot eyes traced her meaty body. She bared her teeth, and it backed away.

"Do sharks like humans?" Lanlan asks.

"We taste like chicken," Kitty says. "Everything tastes like chicken."

"Not to sharks."

Kitty shrugs. She is not seeking answers, which infuriates Lanlan.

Every weekend Lanlan's father drives his electric SUV loaded with scuba-diving equipment to Sanctuary Cove. He is passionate about nature now. He has never cared much about nature until he became a partner at an accounting firm. He used to litter. He used to spit on the streets. But now he counts his carbon footprints the same way he counts taxes, with a delicate balance of intuition and skill. He whitens his teeth and oils his sleek, black hair. He still speaks with an accent, but the townspeople consider it charming. He is exotic and successful, which is why Kitty loves him.

Lanlan doesn't think she can swim. She barely knows how to float.

"But that's perfect," Kitty says.

#

The first time they go scuba-diving, Lanlan and her father have to take a safety class. Kitty has a license already, but she sits with them anyway.

They all change into wetsuits and huddle around the deeply tanned instructor. Lanlan's wetsuit is a size too small, and it binds her body like a second layer of skin threatening to replace the original.

The instructor teaches them some hand gestures to use underwater and tells them that pain in the ears is normal. It is just your body warning you that you are not supposed to be there. But it is okay for them because they are well-equipped.

Lanlan goes down with Kitty and her father with the tanned instructor. Her father sinks without hesitation. It takes Lanlan much longer, but she finally gives in and lets Kitty lead her down.

The world is unbearably blue. Kitty is blue, the fish are blue, even her father is blue, waving to her just a couple of steps away. She wants to wave back, but the water is so heavy that she can't lift her arms. Kitty points at the swarms of shining fish, and Lanlan can see her smiling eyes through the goggles. It is as if Kitty is introducing Lanlan to her family for the first time.

Lanlan watches the fish zooming by. Hello. Bubbles rise from her mouth. It is quiet, and her own breathing is disturbingly loud. It is embarrassing. The fish are looking at her funny. They swerve around her to avoid collision. They know she does not belong here. They know her webbed feet and sleek skin are fake. Heat burns on Lanlan's cheeks.

Kitty wants to lead her deeper, but Lanlan stops her and points up. I must not impose, Lanlan thinks.

She has never gone scuba-diving again.

#

Lanlan now stays at home on weekends when her father and Kitty are underwater. They get a nanny to watch her, Granny Chen. Granny Chen has lived on the island for a long time. She might even die here, whether she likes it or not. Her house is not far from Sanctuary Cove.

"There used to be a lighthouse on the cove. Right at the end of the hill," she tells Lanlan.

"What happened to it?"

"Gone. Wasted away. Its stump is still there."

The stump haunts Lanlan in her dreams. She is afraid of becoming the same. She is afraid of losing her legs. She dreams of broken kneecaps.

"Yield!" she yells in her dreams.

Granny Chen suggests that she think of happier things before bed.

"What do you want to be when you grow up?"

She wants to be a book on a nightstand with a cherished leaf pressed in its pages. She wants to be a Taoist nun. She wants to be a green candle light flickering near an ancient Buddha carved from one single stone.

But Lanlan does not share this.

"What are the stories your mother used to read you? Where is she?" Granny Chen persists.

"She's gone to a place far away."

"Oh, dear. I'm sorry."

"She's not dead," Lanlan explains. "She has actually gone somewhere far away."

"Oh. I'm sorry."

"She writes. She sends postcards with pre-printed greetings. She signs them. I think she is suffering. Maybe it is not her who has gone to a faraway place. It is us. She would tell people, 'My husband and child are somewhere far away,' and they would think we were dead. But we are alive and well, here on this island, with Kitty Cassidy, scuba-diving."

"It is dreadful to be underwater."

"You are right. We shouldn't overstay our welcome."

#

Granny Chen invites Lanlan to her house by the cove. She has a room with a giant light in it. Its face is round and bright red. It used to be on top of the lighthouse, and it has seen many boats home.

The light has always been enlightened. It has never had the privilege of being lost. It is exactly where it should be.

Granny Chen and Lanlan sit in the light's room in the late afternoon. It is the light's favorite time of the day. It remembers when it was still shining over the ocean as the sun slowly lost its grip and boats with furled sails drifted lazily to the harbor.

"These are my twin sons," Granny Chen shows Lanlan a picture of two young men. They are frowning at the camera as if the sun were in their eyes. They each have a folded ear.

"What's with their ears?"

"They used to share an ear when they were in my belly. The doctor had to cut them apart."

Lanlan can't help but feel envious of such a relationship. How fantastic it is to share something as intimate as hearing with somebody who looks exactly like you.

"I think my father has trouble hearing," Lanlan says. "One time, I slept over at my friend's place, but I had a bad dream so I wanted to go home. I called him in the middle of the night. He picked up. I heard the shuffling of mahjong in the background, the click click click of plastic tiles like water dripping from a loose faucet. I was screaming to the receiver, Lanlan, I told him, it's Lanlan! But he kept screaming back, What? What! Maybe I had the wrong number. I couldn't tell if it was his voice now that I think of it."

"There, there," Granny Chen says.

#

Lanlan's father gets his scuba-diving license. He puts it in the see-through plastic pocket within his wallet and carries it close to his chest. Kitty smiles at this. Lanlan knows certain things cannot be helped.

Kitty and Lanlan's father take Lanlan to the cove again, because Granny Chen is no longer available.

"She is dead," Kitty tells Lanlan.

"Dead!"

"Yes. Quite dead. She was a lot sicker than she looked."

"Are the twins here?"

Apparently they are not. No one is here. It is said that she had no family.

Lanlan sits on a bench on the beach with binoculars. Kitty wants her to try diving again, but she politely declines. She points her binoculars to the sea and sees her father and Kitty's bobbing heads. She sees whales and large, white plastic bags in the distance. In a second, they are all gone, submerged in the hungry blue waves.

#

The weather vane whispers to Lanlan at night. She is having trouble sleeping. She is worried sick about the light in dead Granny Chen's house, all by itself. Even though it is enlightened, it still needs looking after.

She begs her father to take her to Granny Chen's house again so that she can visit the light.

Lanlan's father can never say no to her.

The house is not locked. Lanlan goes to the light's room. It regards Lanlan with curiosity, but it knew that she would return. It is sad because it has nothing to offer her. They are two puzzle pieces of the same shape, so they cannot fill each other's void. Lanlan, too, knows this, and she does not blame the light. She understands that the universe acts without intent.

She finds the picture of the twins and folds it into her pocket.

#

A week after Granny Chen dies, a lawyer visits Lanlan's father. He tells him that Granny Chen has left her house to Lanlan.

Lanlan's father is overjoyed. He can see ways it can generate profits and tax savings. Kitty weeps at this. They will tear the house down and build something new. They will have their own summer home here on this island. They will rent it out the rest of the year to men and women with cotton shirts and drawstring pants, who are confident and relaxed, on land and in water. They will paint it blue.

Lanlan wants none of these things. She briefly considers leaving and taking to the sea, then shudders at the thought of the rootless water. If it were up to her, she'd like to have strings running everywhere in the house, connecting to things. She'd like to tie little bells on the strings, so when she drifts through the house in the blindness of the night, the crisp ringing of the bells can lead her to her destination.

But it is not up to her, so Lanlan only asks to save the light.

Her father engages an architect for the new house. It will have an abundance of potted plants, a glass ceiling that hoards the sun. It will blur the boundary between outside and inside. It will certainly have no bells and therefore offer no guidance.

The light will go into the attic, accessible only through a spiral stairwell twirling to the top. Its red face will peek from the round window under a slanted roof, facing the Atlantic.

Lanlan insists on sleeping in the same room with the light. She longs to be with somebody who understands and accepts. They share no home nor happiness, but they can at least keep each other safe.

Together, they will look out to the sea where luckier and less enlightened beings roam.

The Doctor Says Roots Are Growing Around Her Heart

And that is why she feels the pain. It's not really a pain, she says. It's more like a slow burning, like when you cook braised pork feet, you have to keep the stove on low heat, so low that only a flicker of glow remains. We'll have to cut them out, the doctor says. But I've always had them, she says. Always lived with the burn. It's bad for you. See it for yourself. The x-ray shows her caged heart, nested in the embrace of twining arms. She has never seen it before, never seen the inside of her body like an out-turned pocket. During the surgery, she dreams. The roots rope around her. They whisper in a language she no longer speaks and they sing of a distant, forgotten land and all the while they burn.

But the burning is retreating, branches recoiling. Her dreams roll back, an ebbing tide. She wakes. Her body is light, like duckweed drifting on dead water. The clean and untangled heart moans within her as she returns to life with a hollow hope. Later, when she is old and lay dying, she feels under her left breast the scab of a slit and yearns for a rope that will once again pull her home to the shore of soothing burns.

Heritage

She centers a tear-drop jade pendant on a silk scarf, folds the four corners on top of each other, flips it, and ties it up with a gold string. She admires her neat packaging, pats it twice with her fingertips, then slips it in the tiny inner pocket of her handbag, perfect for its size. On the fourteen-hour flight from Shanghai to Los Angeles, she reaches inside the bag and feels the comfortable weight of the small stone.

On her daughter's wedding day, she dons her red qipao, pressed in early morning after a sleepless night, smooth like a mirror. Her daughter wears white, as is customary in a Western wedding.

Before the ceremony, she strings the pendant through a red thread and puts it around her daughter's neck. The tear-drop stone sets right at the dip of her collarbone, marbled by smokes and fogs of soft green.

When her daughter stands at the altar, next to a straw-haired man, in front of somebody else's god, she notices that the jade is tucked behind the lace of her daughter's white dress.

#

Almost a hundred years earlier, a young woman steps off a green-skinned sleeper train in Shanghai. In her hand she clutches a telegram, which she shows to one of the rickshaw pullers loitering in front of the station.

It's plum rain season and a curtain of drizzle falls as they race on the streets, next to trolleys, bicycles, and motor cars. Strange buildings loom on both sides of the road, with round domes and curved facades, like fat giants with protruding bellies. She stares at the foreigners walking in and out of those buildings, men in wide-brimmed hats and women with white, laced umbrellas.

They arrive at the gate of a university. The young woman pays the puller with three coins she fishes out from the hidden pocket inside her coat.

She stands by the gate and waits for her husband. They've been married for five years, and this is the second time she is meeting him. She doesn't quite remember his face, for the first time she was under a red wedding veil most of the night, staring down at her silk shoes.

Her husband left the morning after for his studies in university. He is a modern man with modern ambitions, and in need of a modern wife. A month ago he telegraphed her, informing her that their marriage is annulled and he has proposed to another. Before they part ways, can she please return the family heirloom?

A week before boarding the train, she bought a cheap replica of the tear-drop pendant. His new bride will not wear the jade that warmed her skin and bore her hopes.

She smiles in secret triumph as a man calls out her name.

#

Three centuries before, a mother crouches in the shrubs across from a Western temple, watching and waiting. The sun is climbing up, painting a small bundle on the doorsteps in gold.

The mother walked all night to town with her newborn girl strapped in front of her chest. She picked up a tree branch as a staff, leaning on it now and then to rest. Even at night, the air felt sluggish and the heat weighed her down. The drought withered most of their crops, and they have already emptied the storage. This winter will be long and dark, although coldness seemed a welcoming prospect as she stumbled on the dirt road, sweat burning her eyes.

Her neighbor, who is also a mother, told her that a foreign monk in town takes in babies. The god they worship is a woman, she said, a woman holding a baby. Theirs must be a merciful god.

On the wrist of her girl, she tied a tear-drop jade pendant. It is what's left of her dowry, which she hid from her husband. She imagines one day, many years later, if she is lucky enough to grow old, she will run into a young girl on the street, wearing a silk skirt and a modest smile, with a tear-drop jade on her delicate wrist.

Suddenly, a beggar walks up to the bundle, snatches the jade, and dashes into an alley. The mother freezes. When she is about to rush across the street, the door of the temple opens, and out steps a strange-looking man with deep-set eyes, bluer than the sky above. The mother watches, immobile, as he picks up the baby and disappears behind the door, without the one thing that might bring the girl back to her again.

#

Over a thousand years earlier, a scattered line of riders slumped on camel-back advances westward on the Silk Road. Night falls on the desert, strips the heat from the sand, and hangs an over-sized moon halfway in the black sky. A ghostly wind howls in the distance.

Among the travelers is a maid wrapped in linen from head to toe. Her body sways with the animal that bears her. She has lost count of how many days they've been on the road and knows lesser still how many more they must go.

Her throat burns. The wonder of freedom is wearing off.

An orphan raised within the walls of the palace, she had never seen the world beyond the iron gates of the royal city. Her opportunity came when the emperor assigned her to accompany the princess on her journey to wed a foreign king. Marriage in exchange for peace. She'd been eager to see the sky uninterrupted by the fly-away eaves.

The sky in the desert is boundless. It folds her in, ever-stretching, ever-rolling.

A thump pulls her out of a daze. The princess has fallen. The procession stops. Envoys and servants crowd around the bride. A trembling finger is placed under her nostrils, and a gasp says it all.

The maid stares at the dead princess, then starts to strip her. Angry reproaches are fired, but she pays them no heed. In a moment, it dawns on everyone that the journey must go on, war must be averted, and a princess matters not.

The new princess climbs on the camel, wearing the old princess's clothes and jewels. In her hair, set at the head a silver pin, is a tear-drop jade.

#

Five thousand years ago, a young concubine sits in front of her bronze mirror. Her brows are dyed, hair oiled, and face powdered. A jade pendant hangs around her neck, sculpted in the shape of a teardrop, a token from her mother. She looks almost as beautiful as she did on her wedding day, when she was carried away from her tribe as a gift to the aging emperor.

Outside her window, a pear tree blooms. White petals cascade in the soft breeze of spring, twirling as they fall. She is reminded of fresh snow from her homeland, which she hasn't seen for years.

She dabs on a crimson-colored paste and paints her lips with a shaking hand. The faint wailing in the distance moves closer and closer. She takes a deep breath and walks out of her room, steps towards the road, and kneels on the stone not yet dried from last night's rain. Her white mourning dress drags on the ground, soiled in the muddy water.

The emperor's funeral procession passes before her, and she bows down, her forehead to the cold ground. A dull pain grows each time her head hits the stone. A servant at the end of the procession drops a strip of white silk at her feet. She flinches, shuts her eyes, and feels with her fingertips the chill of the smooth silk.

She stumbles back to the room and picks a spot facing the window. With a swing of her arm, up the silk strip goes, around the wooden beam across the ceiling. She stands on a stool, ties the two ends of the strip together, and pauses.

As she watches the dancing petals, she imagines she is once again home.

#

For millions of years, the jade sleeps inside a green mountain. Not yet found, shaped, or polished.

She bears no significance, and shoulders no great
desires or regrets. Before she is to be passed from
hand to hand, country to country, generation to
generation, she lies innocently in her shell, until one
day an outsider's ax rips her open.

Perfect Vision

Years ago, I rode on my father's shoulders at a pet market. Vendors with cages of animals lined the sidewalk, small rodents spinning in wheels, a black German Shepherd pacing and drooling.

"How far can you see?" My father asked.

"All the way to the end," I said. "Birds!"

I had perfect vision then, and above the bobbing heads I saw wings of rainbow flashing, blue, yellow, red.

We walked towards it, but I don't remember whether we reached the end, or if we did, were there any birds.

#

The loss of my perfect vision was sudden. One day I woke up, and the wooden panes on the window became blurry. I always thought the window strange. It didn't open to the outside, instead it just opened to another room, where my mother slept. It was also built high up, inches from the ceiling, so no one can really look through it.

Everything in my world had a halo, with smudged edges, like I was living in a public bath, where steam softened the outlines of naked strangers.

I had to squint my eyes in school and a boy at the first row thought I was winking at him. He blushed and bowed his head. The curve of his neck reminded me of a swan.

I knew my eyes were getting worse when I saw my father after school one time. He was standing at the gate, along with other parents picking up their kids.

"I thought it was him," I told my mother.

She was busy making pigeon stew.

"I couldn't see his face clearly," I continued. "But I thought it was him."

"Pigeons are good for your eyes," she said. "Pigeons fly. All flying things have good eyes."

#

When my vision deteriorated, my mother finally took me to a doctor. In front of me was a mirror which reflected the eye chart. The mirror doubles the distance, the doctor explained. Things are further away when you look into a mirror. He switched lenses in and out of the heavy set of testing glasses that caged my face. Their legs dug into the skin behind my ears.

I didn't want to wear glasses. I suspected the swan boy wouldn't like me with them.

The doctor told my mother that we could try O.K. Glasses.

"What's that?" she asked.

"If she wears them overnight, she'll have perfect vision during the day."

It was expensive, though. Since my father left, we didn't have much money. My mother had to work again. She was not as beautiful as before, so instead of the starry-eyed girl roles, she now played side characters. The girls' moms, for example. We'd watch TV late at night, for her shows usually aired past prime time.

It was strange watching her play somebody else's mother. She enjoyed the shows, but they bored me.

"Look, Zhenzhen," she would say, "This is the best part." It was always during a crying scene that she said this. She loved watching herself cry. As her character teared up on the screen, she would tear up herself, a single drop rolling down her cheek, a perfect reflection.

#

I started wearing glasses. Everything became clear again, as if I had perfect vision, but of course it was only an illusion, which I resented. When I looked into the mirror, the lenses cut a jagged line on my cheeks as I turned to the side. A Picasso painting.

A memory came to me through a dream. I had forgotten about it, lost it somehow, but it popped up to the surface again like cooked dumplings. I had stolen my father's glasses and put them on my face, walking around feeling wise, until I hit my head on a glass door like a sparrow. The lenses were not made for my eyes, which didn't need correction.

I wondered if it was a curse. I wore his glasses then, and I was granted my own now.

"It's in your genes," my mother said, "Your father's genes. He had terrible eyes."

#

My mother and I took the train to Shanghai for a role she got, which would pay good money, enough for me to get the O.K. Glasses.

"What's the show about?" I asked.

"Big people stuff," she said. She referred to most things as "big people stuff," which "little people" like me wouldn't understand.

"You have a small part in it, too."

"Me?" But I disliked acting, the same way I disliked mirrors.

"Don't fret. You'll have fun."

I heard excitement in her voice, but couldn't see her expression because her face was wrapped in a headscarf and her eyes hid behind large, black sunglasses. She always covered up well in public, especially in crowded places. People might recognize her, she told me. She used to be on calendars and magazine covers; everybody had a picture of her and wanted her autograph on it. At home, in our living room, a poster of her in a large feathered hat hung on the wall. The setting sun glared on it every afternoon, fading the color.

She didn't take off her coverings for the whole trip, even when the conductor came around to check our tickets.

#

The show turned out to be an interview, set in a small auditorium with rows of chairs ascending the stairs. The room was round, dark, and hollow like the inside of a monster's belly.

On the stage, my mother and I sat side by side on a sofa across from the host. I was nervous before I went on stage, but my mother told me that everything was rehearsed beforehand, scripted, even the people in the audience were actors. All I had to do was say yes when she squeezed my hand.

"So it's not a real show then," I said.

She laughed. "Not all you see is real or true, you know. And if you're that worried, just don't wear your glasses."

I took her advice.

Everything was blurry again, which both scared and soothed me. The audience hid in an anonymous darkness, invisible.

The host and my mother talked about her acting career from a decade ago. Then he asked about my father.

"You haven't seen him for…how long?"

"Years."

"Will you see him again? If he was here?"

"What do you mean?"

My mother sat up, and she squeezed my hand.

"Yes!" I blurted out.

The host was pleased that I supplied the line. Music started to play and onto the stage walked a tall figure. I couldn't see his face clearly without my glasses, but for a split second I thought it was my father.

"You…you're here!" My mother gasped.

She was never a good actress, I always thought. Maybe because she was my mother, and I'd seen her real face. Once she gasped, I knew it was not him.

I stared at the stranger, his features a brush of bland color, no eyes, nose or mouth—a cloud of nothingness. He stepped towards us, and my mother flew into his embrace. She dragged my arm with her as she went. I stumbled and almost fell.

She pushed my head onto the stranger's chest, while throwing her arms around his neck. His warm beating heart thumped against my ear. He smelled faintly of smoke and gasoline, which was intoxicating. I felt his large hand on top of my head, stroking my hair. I couldn't decide if I was more revolted or comforted by his touch.

My mother's face nested right next to mine, inches from my impaired eyes, and I didn't remember the last time I saw her this close. Tears marred her cheeks and hung on her eyelashes, like little pearls unstrung. She became younger, more beautiful, and less like my mother.

I choked on my own spit and started coughing, which forced tears to my eyes as well. My mother squeezed my hand again and I said, "Y-yes!"

Applause thundered from the audience and confetti fell all around us.

#

The O.K. Glasses were a scam. It helped in the first couple of months, but my vision gradually reverted back.

"You can never fool yourself for too long," my mother said, although she continued to make pigeon stew.

She never had to wear glasses, however. Only those sunglasses, which were not for seeing.

#

Over the years, I've grown used to my glasses. I startle myself sometimes when I see my face without them.

I want to see things clearly, at all times, so I only take them off when I go to bed.

I imagine in my dreams, I'd still have perfect vision, and if I had to look to the end of a street, or the end of anything, I'd still see wings or rainbows. But I don't dream very often, or if I do, I don't remember them.

8. *And I have never seen such savage delight since*

1. Long ago, we drove in the woods.

2. It was night. My mother was at the wheel, the headlights conjuring shape-shifting wraiths drifting in the darkness.

3. Something flashed like a curse. We stopped.

4. My mother walked in front of the car.

5. I watched through the windshield.

6. It started with her ears. Twitching and lengthening. The back, bowed and bent and balled. The hair, swallowing her bare skin, her arms, her legs, her head, and her whole body, everything shrinking and shaking and shining.

7. She looked back at me, eyes mad and wild and alive.

The Warrior

When she takes off her shoes and steps into the Dojo; when she sheds her dress, the soft shell peels off her skin; when she winds a long, white band around her breasts before slipping into the Keikogi, its wide sleeves cut at her elbows; when she pulls the Hakama up her legs, tying the night-blue belt into a butterfly, tucking the wings just under her waist; when her hands reach into the Kote, the wrinkled leather cool to the touch; when she straps the Do in front of her torso, the hard and comfortable armor hugs her body like a lover; when she puts her head inside the Men, hiding her face behind the metal cage; when she wraps her gloved hands around the Shinai, the length of the sword extends before her; when she takes her stance, right foot forward, left heel lifted, the hem of her Hakama swishing on the springwood floor; she finally feels in Power. She could be Anybody—she could be Born Here, she could be a Man, she could be White, and people would be in *her* Mercy, for once.

Rabbit

Years ago, his mother brought home a rabbit.

"Make it fat, will you?" she asked him.

The boy held the shivering rabbit in his arms, wrapped it in his coat, folded its body into his, feeling the weak tremble next to his heart. It was spotless and white like fresh snow.

On his way back from school every day, he collected weeds from the side of the streets. It ate them quietly, with a quivering mouth. Sometimes the boy could catch a glimpse of those big front teeth chewing on the green.

It never made much sound, which the boy liked.

#

One day, when the boy came home, his mother had made soup.

"Eat up. It's good for you." She filled the boy's bowl with meat and broth.

The meat was tender, falling off the bone.

"Fatty, isn't it?"

The boy paused and looked at his mother, then stared at the soup. Chunks of pink meat floated in it. He thought of the warm, mute snowball against his chest.

"You already had two bowls. Wasn't it good?"

Yes. It was good. The boy thought he'd be sick, but he only felt full.

His father's new wife had a small daughter. She didn't like it whenever the boy went to their home.

"My dad hates you," she told him. "Both you and your mama."

She loved wearing a puffy white dress, with a white hair thing on her head. She had a wide gap between her front teeth.

"Take your sister to play, will you?" his father asked while playing mahjong.

They played badminton at the empty lot next to the apartment. There was a bicycle shed by the lot, about two-story high. Every time the bird went on top of the shed, the boy climbed up to get it.

"I want to go up this time," the daughter said after the bird went up again.

"It's dangerous."

"I don't care. I'm going."

She climbed up.

He didn't know she'd fall. It was her own fault, of course. He told her it was dangerous.

She hurt her head, the boy heard, never quite the same. His father didn't let him see her again.

A matchmaker once introduced a vegetarian woman to him. She wore a string of sandalwood Buddha beads around her wrist. When she talked, she fiddled with them nonstop.

She asked him if he'd ever thought about giving up meat. He told her it was too hard.

Sometimes he feels guilty about the loosened step on top of the bicycle shed. But it never lasts long.

Herd

She became a resident at The Gift in March, when she had six months left, and now it is June.

"June!" A woman says to Yanzi at the weekly gathering, "How horrid. Do you know that my husband died in June. That is the only upside. Other than that, it is horrid."

Yanzi does know it, for she's told her about him the first time they met, sitting under a palm tree by her mobile home. The Gift is full of mobile homes, most of them painted in pleasant pastel colors as if they were Easter eggs scattered on protected grass, waiting for some children to find them.

The husband was a mechanic at an oil field. He fell into one of the tanks filled with a colorless, odorless, lethal chemical.

"There is a god," the woman declares. "He watches from seven feet above."

Others nod their agreement.

"We are the lucky ones," the leader of the

gathering says. He is a priest of some sort, a devout man with unwavering beliefs. Yanzi thinks of him inappropriately naive.

"I hear that elephants know when they are near the end. They would walk away from their herd and go somewhere else to die," a young girl says. She is in a bright, traditional dress with sleeves that drape like a soft waterfall.

"Is a group of elephants called a herd?" Someone asks.

"I think herd is more for sheep…"

"Anything that doesn't know where it's going can be called a herd."

"But if the elephant knows…"

The discussion goes on for about half an hour until dinner is served. Yanzi goes to the gathering mainly for the food. She is tired of cooking and eating alone, but she is too hungry to skip meals altogether. In that sense, she still lives. Her will is either too strong or not strong enough.

The food served at the gathering is of a good variety. They get decent Chinese food sometimes, which is alarmingly close to the real thing. They get Peruvian or Thai or Ethiopian other times, which by the same logic should also be almost-authentic. That is all one can ask for at The Gift.

Yanzi is content. She doesn't really want something accurate or genuine, which can be insensitive and cruel. One time they ordered pho, and one of the residents fainted from just smelling the broth. Yanzi is glad it wasn't anything she has secretly hoped for. Who knows what would happen to her then? She doesn't want to embarrass herself in front of her new neighbors, who are her last companions.

#

At The Gift, it is always summer. The landscaping in the community is professionally done by a company called The Yard Brothers, and they come every Thursday to cut the grass and shape the bushes. Two men drive a white van from home to home, tending to the healthy and hopeful plants outside. The company's logo is stamped on the side of the van, a large, round design. A flower sits at the fork of the "Y" like a crown. Below it, two lines of bolded texts say "We have help, call us," followed by a number.

Yanzi watches the van every week from her window. One of the men, one of the brothers, always waves at her. He later introduces himself as Jay.

He was born and raised in the town, he tells her.

"Have you ever thought about leaving?" She asks.

"I've got everything here, don't I?"

Yanzi is shocked and confused. She has never felt she's got everything anywhere. What she lacks is nameless and cannot be obtained by ordinary means.

When Yanzi was a little girl, she used to steal from a stationary store. It wasn't anything serious. She only took things that no one would miss. She stole a heart-shaped lock from a diary. She stole a small, spotted dog made of porcelain. She stole a miniature pipe the size of her pinkie.

"But we are all guilty of certain desperation," she explains.

"Some trees can only survive in this climate," Jay says. "This is a good town for trees."

"Do you think you can plant a willow tree outside my home?" Yanzi asks.

"That's not local."

"You said it's good for trees here."

Jay frowns at Yanzi as if she had insulted him.

Yanzi goes back to her mobile home and resumes watching the brothers from the window. The white van reflects and redirects the harsh sunshine.

Yanzi thinks of earthworms drying on sidewalks after rain. The audacity of it, the despair.

It hasn't rained for many days.

#

At the end of July, Izaya moves into the baby blue mobile home next to Yanzi. He is a literary type. He wrote books and gave talks at universities. The books line the mahogany shelf in his living room, their spines beautifully hard and straight, climbed by fonts that command a certain authority.

"They will be my legacy," He says more to himself than to Yanzi.

"Of course," She obliges.

Izaya is confident that people would want to know his stories, that they are curious and kind. Yanzi indulges this fantasy. It is why she likes him, for we all need someone to remind us of the brighter side of things, whether or not there is indeed such a side.

She picks up cooking again. She used to cook for her husband, who often worked late. She would cover the dishes with a lime green food net to keep out fruit flies. Sometimes she'd fall asleep waiting, but always woke at the crisp sound of a key turning in its matching lock. He's home, she would think with such breathless panic and glee.

Izaya tolerates Yanzi's cooking, but he'd rather eat elsewhere.

"You have to move on," he says.

He takes Yanzi to a fancy restaurant in town. Yanzi hasn't eaten anything outside of The Gift for months. Food outside is not for her, not in many ways, of that she is certain.

There is a long line outside of the restaurant. It loops around the corner even, and some people have chairs and tents with them.

"It's very popular," Izaya says proudly.

Yanzi doesn't mind the wait. She is used to waiting. She is never in a hurry.

"You can eat the knives and forks," Izaya says. "They serve a dish that is pickled pigskin on a tree trunk. A tree truck made of glass made of sugar made of mermaid tears."

"Mermaid tears are for longevity," Yanzi says.

Izaya is not amused.

#

The priest who leads the gatherings at the Gift is not one of the residents, although he has always referred to himself as "we."

We are the lucky ones.
We are together.
Shall we?

It offers a sense of inclusiveness, which is of course false, but at least he has good intentions. He is warm and courteous to the residents. He is a good man, an upright man, who has their best interest at heart, although Yanzi knows that he would not hesitate to hurt or kill them under different circumstances.

The priest is eager to have Yanzi buy into something.

"There is still a long way ahead of us," he says.

"In the heaving hills of Southern China, where the ground is covered by ferocious greenery, there is a clan of people who always bury their dead near home," Yanzi tells him.

The priest leans forward for the story. He thinks he is close to crack her.

"A shepherd of the dead would travel all over the country to bring back his deceased kinsmen. He would stand them up, tie them next to one another with ropes around their waists, and lead them back into the hills with a gentle tug."

"A shepherd," the priest says.

"Sometimes, the walk back can take years, decades."

The priest has tears in his eyes.

"But there is a distance one cannot walk."

The priest yelps weakly.

Yanzi gets up for a second round of food. The priest trails behind her, looking for guidance.

#

Yanzi often keeps her windows open, but there is seldom any wind. The sun stands still in her brief home.

Outside, a commotion starts, and people are shouting with either excitement or horror, Yanzi couldn't tell which.

"All aboard the trouble bus!" Someone cheers.

Is it time for the weekly gathering again? She has lost track of time passing. There is only day and night, the former improbably longer than the latter. She wakes in the morning, utterly oblivious.

But before the colorless light, in the folds of darkness, she too dreams. She too sleeps safe and sound in her shell. She too longs to grow hoofs and horns and wings and leap forward a thousand miles through vast woodlands, along with her brothers and sisters, hurdling towards a destination where she is eagerly, eagerly expected.

"The Stag" originally appeared in *Gulf Coast*. "The Doctor Says Roots Are Growing Around Her Heart" originally appeared in *Passages North*. "The Blue" originally appeared in *Split Lip Magazine*. "A Heart That Does Not Beat" and "You Will Never Need to Walk Again" originally appeared in *Janus Literary*. "Perfect Vision" originally appeared in *Funicular Magazine*. "8. And I have never seen such savage delight since" originally appeared in *100 Word Story*. "Rabbit" originally appeared in *Fractured Literary*. "The Warrior" originally appeared in *Milk Candy Review*. "Heritage" originally appeared in *Baltimore Review*. "Herd" originally appeared in *Tahoma Literary Review*.